Marty Monster

Malorie Blackman
Illustrated by Kim Harley

Tamarind Ltd

Sponsored by **NASUWT**

For Neil and Elizabeth
with love

Danny and June
had been playing
in the garden
all afternoon.

"Dinner in ten minutes,"
called Mum.

"Hey Danny," whispered June,
"we've just got time
to find the Marty Monster."

"But it's dinner time.
The Marty Monster will be hungry,"
said Danny.

"We'll be very careful," said June.

And off they went.

They sailed across
the ocean.

"Look out!
There's a whale!"
Danny pointed.

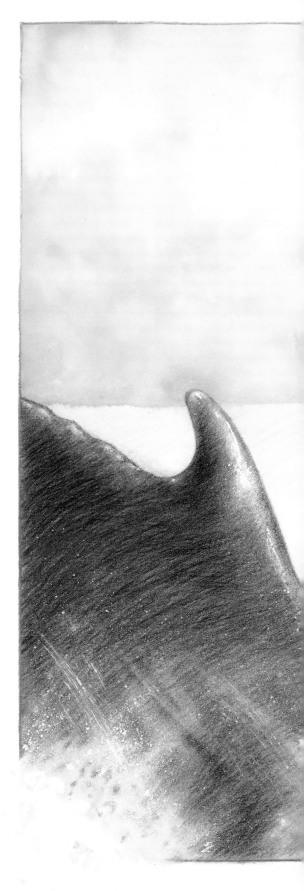

"No problem!" said June.

And she rowed their boat quickly the other way.

They climbed a huge, high mountain.

"Look out for that hungry wolf!"

"Don't worry!" said June.

And she scared it away
with a loud shout.

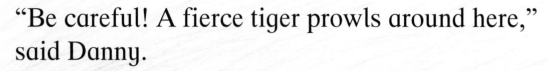

"Be careful! A fierce tiger prowls around here,"
said Danny.

They hid in a cave, to be on the safe side.

The most fierce tiger
in the whole world came past.
Danny and June held their breath
until it had gone.

They tip-toed round
the deep, bubble lake.

They didn't want
to wake up the huge
blubber blob.

"We're almost there," said June. "That's where the Marty Monster hides."

It was the scariest place in the world.

Enter the Dungeon at own risk!

Danny and June crept in.

Luckily, the Monster
was fast asleep and
snoring his head off.

"Let's get him!"
whispered June.

Danny sneaked up
to the Marty Monster.

"DINNER TIME!"
he shouted.

The Marty Monster
sprang up.

"ARRAAGHH!"
he roared.

He chased Danny and June
out of the dungeon,

past the blubber blob,

past the killer cat,

past the hungry wolf,

down,

down,

down

the huge, high mountain…

And into the kitchen.

Dinner was on the table.

"Mind your manners, Marty!"
warned Mum.
"You're such a monster!"

OTHER TAMARIND TITLES

Dizzy's Walk
Mum's Late
Rainbow House
Starlight
Zia the Orchestra
Jessica
Where's Gran?
Toyin Fay
Yohance and the Dinosaurs
Time for Bed
Dave and the Tooth Fairy
Kay's Birthday Numbers
Mum Can Fix It
Ben Makes a Cake
Kim's Magic Tree
Time to Get Up
Finished Being Four
ABC – I Can Be
I Don't Eat Toothpaste Anymore
Giant Hiccups
Boots for a Bridesmaid
Are We There Yet?
Kofi and the Butterflies
Abena and the Rock – Ghanaian Story
The Snowball Rent – Scottish Story
Five Things to Find –Tunisian Story
Just a Pile of Rice – Chinese Story

For older readers, ages 9 – 12
Black Profiles Series
Benjamin Zephaniah
Lord Taylor of Warwick
Dr Samantha Tross
Malorie Blackman
Baroness Patricia Scotland
Mr Jim Braithwaite

A Tamarind Book

Published by Tamarind Ltd, 1999

Text © Malorie Blackman
Illustrations © Kim Harley
Edited by Simona Sideri

ISBN 1 870516 42 7

Designed and typeset by Judith Gordon
Printed in Singapore

In a hospital

Vic Parker

Heinemann
LIBRARY

Little Nippers

www.heinemann.co.uk/library
Visit our website to find out more information about **Heinemann Library** books.

To order:
☎ Phone 44 (0) 1865 888066
▤ Send a fax to 44 (0) 1865 314091
▢ Visit the Heinemann Bookshop at www.heinemann.co.uk/library to browse our catalogue and order online.

First published in Great Britain by Heinemann Library, Halley Court, Jordan Hill, Oxford OX2 8EJ, part of Harcourt Education. Heinemann is a registered trademark of Harcourt Education Ltd.

Editorial: Jilly Attwood and Claire Throp
Design: Jo Hinton-Malivoire and bigtop, Bicester, UK
Models made by: Jo Brooker
Picture Research: Rosie Garai
Production: Séverine Ribierre

Originated by Dot Gradations
Printed and bound in China by South China Printing Company

ISBN 0 431 17320 6 (hardback)
08 07 06 05 04
10 9 8 7 6 5 4 3 2 1

ISBN 0 431 17325 7 (paperback)
08 07 06 05 04
10 9 8 7 6 5 4 3 2 1

British Library Cataloguing in Publication Data
Parker, Vic
In a hospital – (Who helps us?)
610.6'9
A full catalogue record for this book is available from the British Library.

Acknowledgements
The publishers would like to thank the following for permission to reproduce photographs: Custom Medical Stock Photo pp. **8**, **23**; Peter Evans Photography pp. **4**, **5**, **6**, **7**, **9**, **11**, **12–13**, **14–15**, **16**, **17**, **18**, **19**, **20–21**, **22**; Sally and Richard Greenhill p. **10**.

Cover photograph reproduced with permission of Peter Evans Photography.

The publishers would like to thank Annie Davy for her assistance in the preparation of this book.

Every effort has been made to contact copyright holders of any material reproduced in this book. Any omissions will be rectified in subsequent printings if notice is given to the publishers.

2

Contents

Into a hospital 4

Visiting a ward 6

Having an operation 8

Staying in hospital 10

It's an emergency! 12

Ouch! 14

A special machine 16

There, there! 18

Picking up medicine 20

Feeling better 22

Index 24

Into a hospital

Hospitals are busy places.

4

Visiting a ward

receptionist

Have you come to visit a patient?

A receptionist will tell you where to go.

6

Having an operation

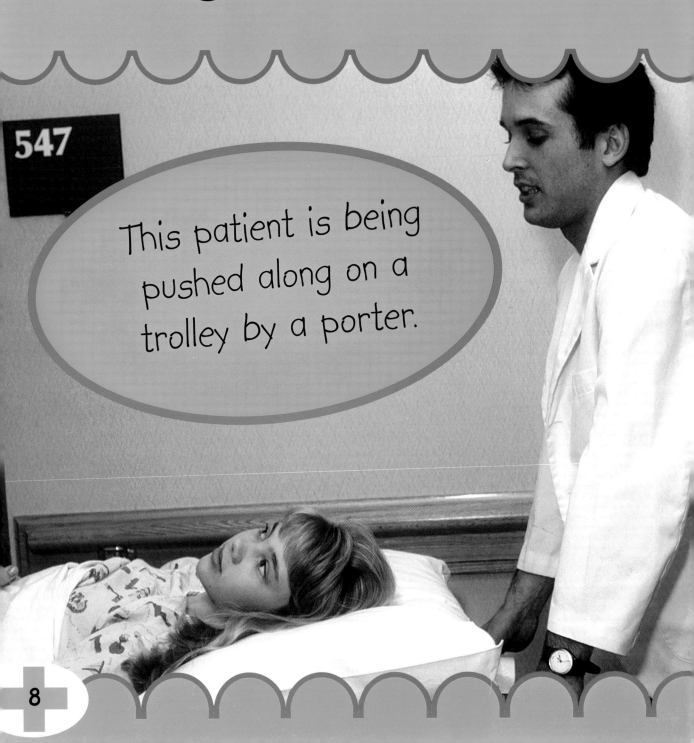

547

This patient is being pushed along on a trolley by a porter.

Staying in hospital

Some hospitals have a school.

teacher

Some hospitals have a radio station too.

This DJ is playing music for everyone.

It's an emergency!

Ne-nah!
Ne-nah!

Here comes an ambulance crew with another patient.

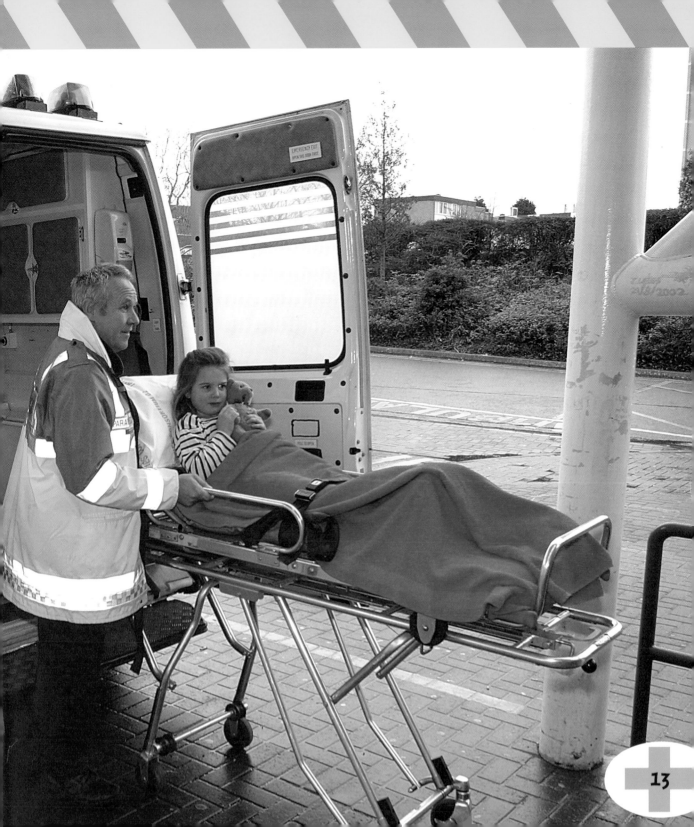

13

The doctor will soon find out by doing special tests.

15

A special machine

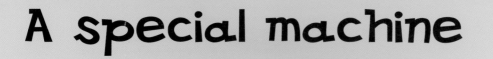

radiographer

This machine photographs inside your body.

16

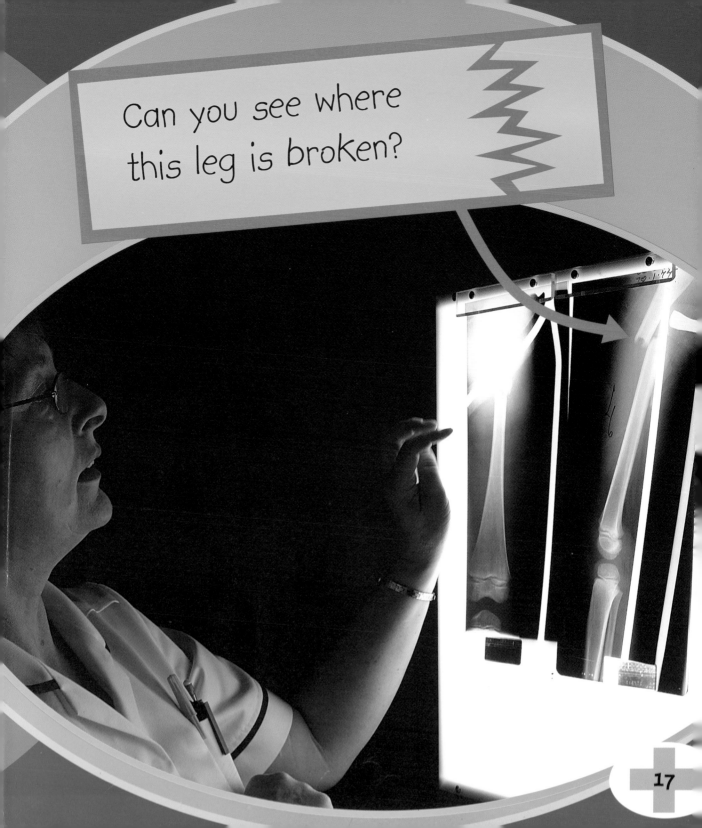

17

There, there!

This **wet** plaster will soon go hard and **stiff**.

It will keep the broken bone **straight** while it mends.

18

Who is helping this patient?

19

Picking up medicine

pharmacist

20

In a hospital, there are lots of different medicines to make you well.

Feeling better

Some people need special exercises to make them better.

physiotherapist

This hospital helper is hard at work too.

Can you guess who it is?

Index

ambulance crew . . 12, 13

doctor 14, 15

nurse 18, 19

pharmacist 20, 21

physiotherapist 22

porter 8

receptionist 6

security guard 5

surgeon 9

The end

Notes for adults

The *Who helps us . . .?* series looks at a variety of people that a young child may come across in different situations. The books explore who these people are, why we might interact with them, and how to communicate appropriately. Used together, the books will enable discussion about similarities and differences between environments and people, and encourage the growth of the child's sense of self. The following Early Learning Goals are relevant to this series:

Knowledge and understanding of the world
Early learning goals for a sense of place:
- show an interest in the world in which they live
- notice differences between features of the local environment
- observe, find out about and identify features in the place they live and the natural world
- find out about their environment, and talk about those features they like and dislike.

Personal, social and emotional development
Early learning goals for a sense of community:
- make connections between different parts of their life experience
- understand that people have different needs, views, cultures and beliefs, which need to be treated with respect.
Early learning goals for self-confidence and self-esteem:
- separate from main carer with support/confidence
- express needs and feelings in appropriate ways

- initiate interactions with other people
- have a sense of self as a member of different communities
- respond to significant experiences, showing a range of feelings when appropriate
- have a developing awareness of their own needs, views and feelings and be sensitive to the needs, views and feelings of others.

This book introduces the reader to a range of people they may come across when at a hospital. It will encourage young children to think about the jobs these people perform and how they help the community. **In a hospital** will help children extend their vocabulary, as they will hear new words such as *operation* and *pharmacist*. You may like to introduce and explain other new words yourself, such as *stretcher* and *x-ray*.

Follow-up activities
- Use a toy doctor's kit to explain and role play routine procedures such as taking a temperature, using a stethoscope, putting on a bandage etc.
- Explain the difference between tablets and sweeties, and that only grown-ups should touch medicines. The child could draw a picture of a doctor or a nurse giving a patient some medicine to make them better.
- Make a toys' hospital with a cardboard cut-out ambulance, shoe box beds and scraps of material for bandages.